AuthorHouse™
1663 Liberty Drive
Bloomington, IN 47403
www.authorhouse.com
Phone: 1 (800) 839-8640

Because of the dynamic nature of the Internet, any web addresses or links contained in this book may have changed since publication and may no longer be valid. The views expressed in this work are solely those of the author and do not necessarily reflect the views of the publisher, and the publisher hereby disclaims any responsibility for them.

Any people depicted in stock imagery provided by Getty Images are models, and such images are being used for illustrative purposes only.
Certain stock imagery © Getty Images.

This book is printed on acid-free paper.

ISBN: 978-1-7283-3350-2 (sc)
ISBN: 978-1-7283-3349-6 (e)

Library of Congress Control Number: 2019917139

Print information available on the last page.

Published by AuthorHouse 01/18/2020

authorHOUSE®

Peachy
The Duck Who Loves Ice Cream

ON THE FARM

MARTIN LATIGUE

My name is Peachy, the City Park Duck that loves ice cream. Last night was my first night in the farm. There were no sounds of cars and busses passing in the night. I was having the best sleep of my life, until morning, when I was awakened by the sounds of cock-a-doodle-do

I ran outside of the barn to find the rooster on a fence post, doing his cock-a-doodle-do. The people in the farm-house heard him too, because the lights in the farm-house came on.

This cock-a-doodle-do, was the wake-up call for all farm life, The chickens would go lay eggs, the rabbits were running around playing.

The cows, the goats and the pigs was waiting on the boss of the farm, Mark, to bring them food for the morning. After feeding all the animals, Mark and I would walk to the pond.

Mark told me his son, Mark Jr. was home today. He had been to college in Texas. He went there to be a veterinarian, an animal doctor. He would take care for all the animals in this farm and help the other farmers.

Mark asked me to talk to his son. I had never talk to anyone but Mark, I agreed to talk to his son. Last night there was a party for Mark Jr., they had cakes and ice cream. I had ice cream only.

The next day, after Mark and Mark Jr. had fed all of the farm animals. They walked with me to the pond. Mark Jr. asked me if could I talk to the other animal, I said I could, but not the way people talk to each other. Animals, express their thoughts, opinions and feelings, by standing in front of each other and looking in each other's eyes and reading each other's thinking

Mark Jr., made the farmers happy with the care he had as a doctor for the animals. He made the sick animals well. I am happy too because I assisted, by talking to the animals and I would assess the faces of the animals to have some ideas on what they were feeling.

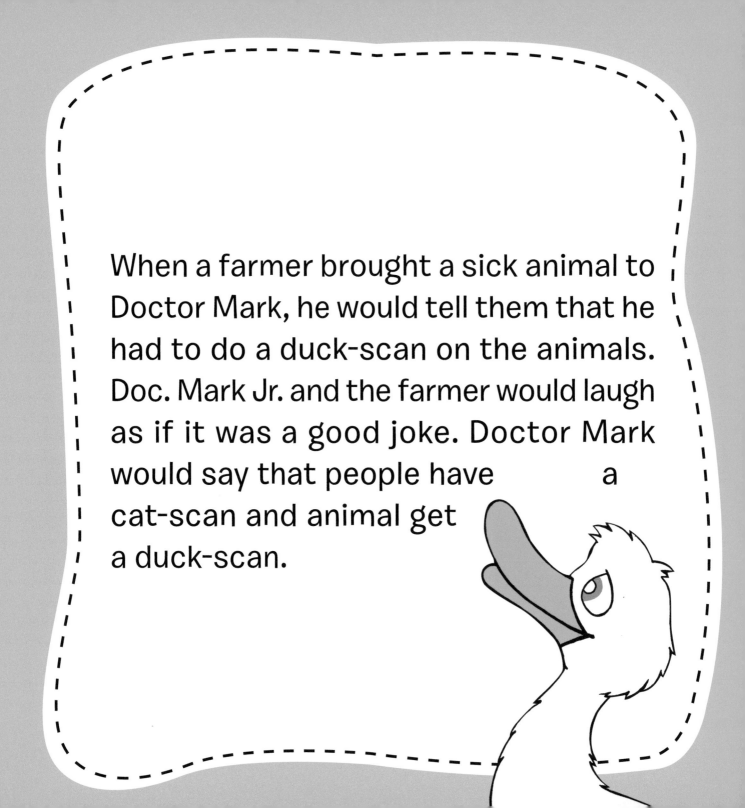

When a farmer brought a sick animal to Doctor Mark, he would tell them that he had to do a duck-scan on the animals. Doc. Mark Jr. and the farmer would laugh as if it was a good joke. Doctor Mark would say that people have a cat-scan and animal get a duck-scan.